HECTOR AND CHRISTINA

Also by Louise Fatio and Roger Duvoisin

THE HAPPY LION

THE HAPPY LION IN AFRICA

THE HAPPY LION AND THE BEAR

THE HAPPY LION ROARS

THE HAPPY LION'S QUEST

THE HAPPY LION'S TREASURE

THE HAPPY LION'S VACATION

THE THREE HAPPY LIONS

THE HAPPY LION'S RABBITS

RED BANTAM

MARC AND PIXIE

HECTOR PENGUIN

To our granddaughter, Anne

Library of Congress Cataloging in Publication Data

Fatio, Louise.
Hector and Christina.

SUMMARY: Hector the Penguin is captured and forced to live in a zoo where he falls in love with another penguin named Christina.

[1. Penguins—Fiction] I. Duvoisin, Roger Antoine, 1904–
II. Title. PZ7.F268He   [E]   77-7086
ISBN 0-07-020072-6
ISBN 0-07-020073-4 lib. bdg.

HECTOR
and
CHRISTINA

by Louise Fatio
pictures by Roger Duvoisin

McGRAW-HILL BOOK COMPANY

NEW YORK • ST. LOUIS • SAN FRANCISCO • AUCKLAND • BOGOTÁ • DÜSSELDORF

JOHANNESBURG • LONDON • MADRID • MEXICO • MONTREAL • NEW DELHI • PANAMA

PARIS • SÃO PAULO • SINGAPORE • SYDNEY • TOKYO • TORONTO

One day Hector Penguin fell off a truck on his way to the zoo. He found himself at the edge of a forest where birds were singing cheerfully. Deep in the forest he came to a pond. Its banks were gay with flowers of all colors. Ducks were swimming on the pond while other animals were busy around it.

How happy Hector was among the friends he found there—the ducks with whom he played in the pond, the heron, the turtle, the rabbit, the squirrel, the owl, the crow, and Nina the dog who came to visit him every day.

He never missed the frozen Antarctic where he was born.

Ah ha! But one day two men came to the pond.

"Here he is, that's him!" one exclaimed, pointing to Hector. "I have searched for him for weeks."

"Are you sure it's the one you lost on the way to the zoo?" asked the other man.

"Of course. Did you ever see a wild penguin living in a forest pond? Let's catch him and bring him to the zoo."

Catch Hector they did, before he had time to jump into the pond. Poor Hector. He ended that day far, far away from the forest pond, inside a little round yard surrounded by a fence. In the middle of the yard was a round pool. A small house stood beside it. In the little house a fine dinner was waiting for him. But he was alone.

The next morning, when he walked around the small pool and saw a crowd of people looking at him over the fence, he felt sad. Where were all his dear friends? The ducks who swam with him in the large pond? And all the others? Where was the beautiful forest full of singing birds?

All day he walked around and around the pool and looked at the people who looked at him.

It was a sad day.

So was the next day and the next day and many more days after that.

One morning, as Hector jumped out of the water after a dive, what did he see, perched on the fence of the pool? A big, black bird who greeted him joyously. It was his forest friend, the crow.

"So here you are, Hector," called the crow. "I knew I would find you. I flew to several zoos searching for you."

"My dear crow," cried Hector, hugging his friend. "I am so happy to see you. And how are all my other friends?"

"They all miss you and worry about you," said the crow. But now that I have found you I will fly back to them and give them the good news. We will see how we can bring you back to us. Good-bye for a while, Hector."

"Good-bye," waved Hector, watching the crow fly away.

For the rest of the day, he danced around the pool smiling at the visitors who smiled at him.

In the forest the crow called a council to decide what to do about Hector. Everyone had an idea and they all talked at once. But Nina the dog talked the loudest.

"I'll fetch Hector," she said. "Nothing to it. Just wait." And she ran off. The crow flew after her to show her the way.

The zoo was far away. When Nina reached it the next day it was nearly dark. Guided by the crow, she jumped over the fence and ran to the little house where Hector was resting.

"Quick, Hector," she whispered. "Sit on my back like a horseback rider. Hold tight."

With Hector on her back, Nina jumped out of the penguin pen and ran through the zoo garden, into the street.

The passers-by stopped in astonishment at the amazing sight.
"Run, run, run!" cried the crow from above.
"Run, run, run!" cried Hector.
Fast, fast, faster, ran Nina.

Alas, the zoo sent an alarm to the police. Blowing their sirens, the police cars rushed out to catch the escaping penguin.

Nina ran so fast that she tripped on a sidewalk and Hector fell, rolling into the street. Before Hector could jump back on Nina, a police car drove up and a policeman picked him up.

Hector was soon returned to his little pen in the zoo.

As for Nina, she fled through the streets with the crow flying above her. In a lonely backyard they found a safe hiding place for the night.

"We can only return to our forest empty-handed," said Nina.

"Yes," replied the crow, "but when we are back we will call a new council to discuss another idea."

And this was done.

But at this new council it was the crow who talked the loudest.

"Listen," he said. "Nina was strong enough to carry Hector but not fast enough to get away. None of us here is both strong and fast enough. I KNOW who is: the six, big swans in the lake of the zoo garden. I will ask them."

When he glided down to the lake, the swans were retiring for the night. But they all listened to the crow's story.

"Poor, lonely Hector," they said sadly.

"I'll carry him back to your forest," promised the biggest swan.

After his thanks, the crow flew over to Hector's pen. But what a surprise awaited him. Hector was no longer alone. He was talking, and even dancing, with another penguin.

"How wonderful," cried Hector when he saw the crow. "I was hoping you would come back soon to meet my dear Christina. She came yesterday to be my companion here. We have many things to talk about. Isn't she lovely? I will never be lonely again."

"Christina is a very pretty penguin indeed," said the crow. "But I came to lead you back to our pond in the forest. Now you seem so happy here that I fear you love this pen."

"No," said Hector. "I love Christina, not the pen. I love her so much I couldn't live without her. But I would be happier to be free in the forest pond with Christina and all my friends than a prisoner in this zoo."

"I'll be happy with Hector wherever he goes," said Christina.

"Hurrah!" exclaimed the crow. "A big swan promised to carry Hector to our forest; another will surely carry Christina."

Although it was dark now, the crow flew off to wake up the swans and tell them the new story of Hector and Christina.

"What a lovely story," the six swans said together. They liked it so much that they *all* wanted to carry Christina to the forest.

"We will be at Hector's pen when the sun rises," they added.

True to their promise, the six swans came.

"*I* will carry Christina," the biggest swan declared.

"You wanted Hector," said another. "I will carry Christina."

"*I* want to carry Hector," said a lady swan.

"Our forest pond is far away," the crow explained. "Each of you should take turns carrying Hector or Christina part of the way."

The six swans agreed. So, Hector climbed on the back of the biggest
swan. Christina got on another swan. "Hold tight!" called the crow,
taking off. The six swans spread out their wide wings and flew off after

him. It was so early in the morning, the zoo and the town were still asleep. The beautiful swans disappeared undisturbed, into the pink horizon.

When they glided down to the side of the pond all the forest friends welcomed them with singing and dancing.

"Two penguins instead of one, and six swans! What a wonderful surprise!" they cried.

The swans and the penguins were surrounded by the ducks, the heron, the owl, the raccoon, the squirrel, the turtle and even other animals who wanted to be part of the celebration. Nina also came from her farm when she heard the hubbub.

"How beautiful to be here again with all of you!" exclaimed Hector. "I hope that Christina will love you as much as I do."

"Our love to pretty Christina," everyone cried.

"And my love to all of you," sang Christina, flapping her wings.

"It is so wonderful here," said the swans, "that we will stay a while before returning to our lake in the zoo."

But in the midst of this joy, the owl hooted a warning that stopped the singing and dancing. "Do not forget," he said, "that the zoo people will come to fetch Hector and Christina."

"We will not let them," everyone cried. "We will hide our two friends in the forest."

There was no need to worry. When the townspeople learned the story of Hector and Christina, how Hector had grieved alone behind the pen fence, how he finally escaped with Christina, they said: "Hector and Christina must be free to live in the forest with their friends. They can never be happy in a pen, even in our nice zoo."

So the town council voted that the two penguins deserved to live in peace in the forest.

To this day the pond is still called *Hector and Christina Pond.*